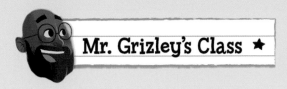

Mr. Grizley's Class ★

# Rahma's

# Gift

by Bryan Patrick Avery    illustrated by Arief Putra

PICTURE WINDOW BOOKS
a capstone imprint

Published by Picture Window Books, an imprint of Capstone.
1710 Roe Crest Drive
North Mankato, Minnesota 56003
capstonepub.com

Library of Congress Cataloging-in-Publication Data is available on
the Library of Congress website.

ISBN: 9781666339123 (hardcover)
ISBN: 9781666339130 (paperback)
ISBN: 9781666339147 (ebook PDF)

Summary: Rahma has a gift for helping friends make up after
arguing. But when her friend Madison gets mad at her, she's not
sure what to do.

Designed by Dina Her

Printed and bound in the USA. PO4882

# TABLE OF CONTENTS

Cecilia Gomez

# Mr. Grizley's Class ★

Shaw Quinn

Emily Kim

Mordecai Foster

Nathan Wu

Ashok Aparnam

Ryan Clayborn

Rahma Abdi

Nicole Washington

Alijah Wilson

Suddha Agarwal

Chad Werner

Semira Madani

Pierre Boucher

Zoe Charmichael

Dmitry Orloff

Camila Jennings

Madison Tanaka

Annie Barberra

Bobby Lewis

## CHAPTER 1

# Not Speaking

Rahma raced into her classroom after recess.

"Am I late?" she asked Mr. Grizley.

Mr. Grizley checked his watch. "Not quite," he said.

"Two kindergartners had an argument," Rahma explained. "I was helping them learn to get along."

Mr. Grizley smiled. "You sure have a gift for doing that," he said.

It was Rahma's turn to smile.
"I just want to help everyone get
along," she said.

Rahma went to her desk and sat down. She tapped her best friend, Madison, on the shoulder.

"You'll never guess what happened at recess," Rahma said.

Madison didn't respond.

"Madison? Did you hear me?" Rahma asked.

Madison turned to Rahma and scowled. "I heard you," she said.

"Why didn't you answer?"
Rahma asked.

Madison turned around.
"Because," she said, "I'm not
speaking to you."

Mr. Grizley passed out math worksheets to everyone in the class.

"Work with a partner on this," he said.

Rahma turned to Annie. "Will you be my partner?" Rahma asked.

"Sure," Annie said. "But don't you want to work with Madison?"

Rahma shook her head. "I'm mad at her," she said. "She's not speaking to me."

## CHAPTER 2

# What to Do?

"Madison is not speaking to you, so you're mad at her?" Annie asked with a frown.

Rahma nodded.

"That doesn't make sense," Annie said.

"Well, I'm not talking to her if she won't talk to me," Rahma said.

"Maybe if you talked to her, you could find out what's wrong," Annie said.

"This doesn't sound like a math discussion," Mr. Grizley said. He stopped next to the girls' desks. Annie nudged Rahma.

"Tell him," Annie said.

"I think Madison is mad at me," Rahma explained. "But I don't even know why."

"Well, if you know she's upset," Mr. Grizley said, "maybe you should work on finding out why."

Rahma looked at Madison. "Maybe you're right," she said.

At lunchtime, Rahma walked around the playground. She thought about her problem with Madison.

"Hey, Rahma!" Chad yelled. He ran over to Rahma. "Thanks for helping Ashok and me work out our argument last week," he said.

"Anytime," Rahma said with a smile. "I'm glad you're friends again. I wish I could fix my problem with Madison."

"Maybe you should take the advice you gave me," Chad said. "Listen to the other person."

"Maybe you're right," Rahma said. "I'll talk to Madison."

# CHAPTER 3

# Fixing a Friendship

Rahma found Madison eating lunch with Semira.

"Madison," Rahma said, "I don't know what I did to make you angry, but I'm sorry that you feel bad."

Madison put down her water bottle. "You made a necklace for Semira," she said.

"Rahma gave me the necklace to help me feel better when my dog was sick," Semira said.

Madison looked surprised.

"I thought you didn't give me one because you didn't want to be my best friend anymore," she said.

"No way!" Rahma said. "I'll always be your best friend."

Madison smiled. "I'm glad," she said.

The bell rang, and the three friends walked to class together.

Mr. Grizley stopped Rahma at the door.

"It looks like you and Madison solved your problem," he said.

Rahma grinned. "You were right," she said. "I just needed to focus on how she felt and why."

# LET'S WRITE AN APOLOGY NOTE

Nobody is perfect. We sometimes make mistakes. Sometimes, the things we do make others feel bad, even if we don't mean to make them feel that way. Rahma went to talk to Madison to apologize for making her feel bad. That's one way to apologize. Another way is to write a note. For this activity, we're going to practice writing a note to say sorry. We'll write a note from Rahma to Madison.

**WHAT YOU NEED:**
- white or colored paper
- pen or pencil (in your favorite color)

**WHAT YOU DO:**
1. Always begin your notes by including the name of the person you're writing to. In this case, you could write "Dear Madison" or "To Madison."

2. This is the really important part of the note. Here, you'll tell Madison why you're sorry. You could write something like "I'm sorry that I did something that hurt your feelings." You might also say something like "I'm really glad you're my friend."

3. Make sure Madison knows who the note is from. You could write "Your friend, Rahma" or just "From Rahma." Do whatever you think is best.

That's it. Not too hard, right? Apologizing is an important part of relationships. Practice writing an apology note from time to time. It's a skill that you'll always be able to use.

# GLOSSARY

**advice** (ad-VAHYS)—suggestions about how to act or what to do about a problem

**argument** (AR-gyuh-muhnt)—a disagreement between two or more people

**discussion** (dih-SKUHSH-uhn)—a conversation or talk to help understand something better

**partner** (PAHRT-ner)—a person who works or does some other activity with another person

**respond** (ri-SPOND)—to say something in return

**scowl** (SKOUL)—to frown

**solve** (SOLV)—to find the answer to a problem

# TALK ABOUT IT

1. At the beginning of the story, Rahma was almost late to class because she was helping two students solve a problem. Have you ever helped someone with a problem? How did you do it?

2. When Rahma tries to talk to Madison, Madison says she is not talking to her. So Rahma decides to ignore Madison. What could Rahma have done instead?

3. Rahma helps many of her schoolmates with their problems. Why do you think she struggles to solve her own problem?

# WRITE ABOUT IT

1. Have you ever had to apologize for something? What did you say? How did your apology make the other person feel? Write about it.

2. In your own words, explain why Madison was upset with Rahma.

3. Rahma's special gift is helping friends make up after they argue. Write about one of your special gifts.

## ABOUT THE AUTHOR

**Bryan Patrick Avery** discovered his love of reading and writing at an early age when he received his first Bobbsey Twins mystery. He writes picture books, chapter books, middle grade, and graphic novels. He is the author of the picture book *The Freeman Field Photograph*, as well as "The Magic Day Mystery" in *Super Puzzletastic Mysteries*. Bryan lives in northern California with his family.

## ABOUT THE ILLUSTRATOR

**Arief Putra** loves working and drawing in his home studio at the corner of Yogyakarta city in Indonesia. He enjoys coffee, cooking, space documentaries, and solving the Rubik's Cube. Living in a small house in a rural area with his wife and two sons, Arief has a big dream to spread positivity around the world through his art.